1/06

Teddy's Cattle Drive

A Story from History

by **Marc Simmons**

illustrations by **Ronald Kil**

University of New Mexico Press • Albuquerque

Books in the Children of the West Series

Millie Cooper's Ride

José's Buffalo Hunt

Friday the Arapaho Boy

Teddy's Cattle Drive

©2005 by Marc Simmons
©2005 illustrations by Ronald Kil
All rights reserved. Published 2005
Printed in Singapore

10 09 08 07 06 05   1 2 3 4 5 6

Library of Congress Cataloging-in-Publication Data

Simmons, Marc.
Teddy's cattle drive : a story from history / Marc Simmons ;
[illustrations by] Ronald Kil.— 1st ed.
p. cm. — (Children of the West series)
Summary: Eleven-year-old Teddy is participating in his first
cattle drive, but when his father leaves him in the hands of the
trail boss, Teddy must prove himself in order to win respect and to
earn his spurs. Based on the memoirs of cowpuncher E.C. Abbott.
ISBN 0-8263-3921-2 (cloth : alk. paper)
[1. Cattle drives—Fiction. 2. Cowboys—Fiction. 3. Responsibility—Fiction.
4. Chisholm Trail—Fiction. 5. West (U.S.)—History—1860–1890—Fiction.]
I. Kil, Ronald R., 1959– ill. II. Title.
PZ7.S591855Te 2005
[Fic]—dc22
                                   2005006291

Series design by Robyn Mundy
Book composition by Damien Shay
Body type is Trump Mediaeval 12.5/22
Display type is Playbill and Giddyup

For
Harlan Hunter Schmaltz
An Old-Fashioned
American Boy

Foreword

Edward Abbott of England came to the United States with his family in 1871. He wanted to start a ranch in the wild West, so he settled in southeast Nebraska.

The buildings and corrals were soon finished. Next he said to his wife: "We're ready now for cattle. I'll go down to Texas and buy a herd of Longhorn cows. Then I'll find cowboys to drive them up the Chisholm Trail to our ranch."

"Why not take Teddy with you," said Mrs. Abbott. Teddy was the youngest son, eleven years old.

"He's too small and sickly for a trip this hard," replied her husband. "I don't think he could make it."

"Remember," added Mrs. Abbott. "The doctor in England told us to keep Teddy in the open air. The outdoor life would be good for him."

Her husband frowned at these words. Mr. Abbott loved his son, though he usually failed to show it. But he doubted that Teddy would ever be much use around the ranch.

Now, however, he agreed with his wife. "All right. Teddy can keep me company," he told her. "And he'll also have a chance to grow up a bit around real cowboys."

Thus, it came about that young Teddy Abbott made his first cattle drive, an experience never to be forgotten.

"Teddy! Teeee-ddy! Come on!" Edward Abbott called loudly to his son. The excited boy galloped up on his new horse.

Mr. Abbott and Teddy rode onto a grassy prairie just below the Red River in Texas. Their journey down from Nebraska by train and boat had taken several weeks.

"Father, when will the cattle get here?" Teddy asked eagerly.

"Anytime, son," answered Mr. Abbott. "The Longhorns I bought three days ago should reach us before noon. Mr. Cross is driving them to us from his ranch."

Vito Cross was a Texas cowman with plenty of know-how. Three times he'd driven a beef herd up the Chisholm Trail.

Now, Edward Abbott had hired him to make another drive north. This time he would deliver a herd to the Abbott ranch in Nebraska.

It was late afternoon before the cattle broke out of the scattered trees onto the prairie. Teddy heard them first, bawling loudly as cowboys shouted and horses whinnied.

Vito Cross rode up to the Abbotts sitting on horseback. Mr. Abbott had purchased two fine riding animals. Teddy's bay horse had a black mane and tail. It was small, but strong and fast. He called him Pete.

On reaching Texas, Edward Abbott had bought his son a big hat, red neckerchief, boots, and a saddle, but no spurs. As Teddy would soon learn, spurs were the mark of a real cowboy, and they had to be earned.

"Sorry I'm late, Mr. Abbott," apologized Vito Cross. "I had a hard time finding a trail crew. But I have it now, and it's a good one."

Teddy watched Mr. Cross's six cowboys closely. They turned the big Longhorns loose on the prairie to graze.

Then suddenly a chuckwagon rolled out of the trees following the cattle. A black man was driving the wagon and its mule team.

Behind came a loose band of horses. They were herded by a couple of young fellows just a few years older than Teddy. They were horse wranglers.

"Well, Mr. Abbott, you can see the whole crew from here," declared Vito Cross. "As trail boss, I will lead the drive."

"The next man in importance is the cook. For that job, I was lucky to hire Mr. Thaddeus. A few years ago, he was a slave. Now, he's the best known range cook in Texas."

Teddy paid careful attention. All the new and strange things fascinated him. "On this drive, I'll soon learn to be a cowboy," he happily thought to himself.

At that moment, Mr. Abbott told his trail boss: "Tomorrow I will see the herd across the Red River into Indian Territory. Then I'll leave you and return to Nebraska by train."

That surprised Teddy. He had supposed that his father would be going on the drive with him. Hearing the news left the boy confused and even angry. "Father didn't tell me he was leaving the herd," he whispered. "What will happen to me?"

Now Mr. Abbott said to Vito Cross: "You'll have to look after my son. Be sure no harm comes to him."

The trail boss nodded his head. But there was a frown on his face. Added to all his other work, he had to serve as nursemaid to a skinny kid who knew nothing about cow horses and Longhorns.

The Abbott crew camped on the edge of the prairie for the night. At dawn they were up and gulping down breakfast fixed by Mr. Thaddeus.

Still sleepy-eyed, Teddy saddled Pete in the half-light. He was excited about facing his first day on the cattle trail. But he was also fearful. Later in the day, he would have to say good-bye to his father.

It was a short drive to the Red River. Mr. Abbott, Teddy, and Vito Cross stopped on the low bank and looked across the wide water. On the other side was Indian Territory. One day it would become the state of Oklahoma.

"The river is not too deep here, but in some places there are bad holes," said Mr. Cross.

"Well, for safety, I want you to tie my son in the saddle when we go over with the herd," replied Teddy's father. "That way he can't fall off and be washed downstream."

Embarrassed, Teddy put his head down. How could his father treat him like a small child, not caring that he had shamed him in front of Mr. Cross?

"Tying your boy is not a good idea," exclaimed the trail boss. "If the river current pulls his horse down, the lad might drown."

Mr. Abbott saw his mistake and allowed Teddy to make the river crossing untied.

"Yip, yip, yip, Ya-a-a-ah," shouted the cowboys.

Swinging coiled ropes over their heads, they pushed the cattle from behind. The animals, led by Vito Cross and Mr. Abbott, plunged into the river's reddish-brown waters and began to swim.

Thrilled by the sight, Teddy shook the leather reins, and his horse Pete followed the last of the Longhorns.

Half way across Red River, Teddy ran into trouble. Here the current was strong. Pete suddenly lost his footing and rolled on his side.

Teddy yelled out in terror as he slid into the treacherous water and went under. In the next moment, he felt a strong hand grab his wrist and pull.

Teddy Abbott popped free of the water to be hauled onto the back of a horse by a grinning cowboy.

"Well, Master Teddy," said his rescuer, "looks like you just took your first bath on the Chisholm Trail."

In spite of his fright, the boy smiled. "I guess, I did," he admitted in a weak voice. "I think I'm gonna wait 'til this cattle drive is over before I take another one."

When the pair got to the north bank of the river, they found Pete already there. He was standing with his head down, water dripping from his nose and from the empty saddle.

Teddy slid to the ground. From horseback, the cowboy reached down to shake his hand. He said: "By the way, my name is Sam. Sam Bass. And I know who you are, of course. You're Mr. Abbott's son."

Then Sam galloped away to catch up with the herd. He left Teddy to climb on his horse and follow.

Instead of mounting Pete, Teddy walked along the riverbank.

"Heck," he said aloud. "Nobody is going to take me serious on this cattle drive. I'm just Mr. Abbott's kid. I even had to be saved from drowning in the river."

From the moment he saw his first cowboys, Teddy knew he wanted to be one of them. But he'd not made a good start. Could he

prove to himself and the others on the drive that he had the stuff to become a cowboy? In the end, would his father care?

Just then he heard a bark. A muddy, skinny dog came out of the bushes by the river. It ran up to Teddy and began to lick his hand.

"Poor hungry thing," Teddy said softly. "Looks like somebody left you behind. Come along with Pete and me. Maybe Mr. Thaddeus can find a bone for you."

The trail cook, indeed, came up with a large beef bone for Teddy's new companion.

"This dog must have gotten lost from some settler's wagon passing by," Mr. Thaddeus guessed. "What're you going to call him?"

"I'll name him Shep," Teddy answered.

Shortly Vito Cross rode up to the chuckwagon. He told the cook to stop just ahead and fix the noon meal for the cowboys.

Then Mr. Cross said: "Teddy, you were late catching up with the herd. Your father left for Nebraska a half hour ago. He asked me to tell you good-bye."

At once the trail boss saw the hurt in Teddy's eyes. He figured Mr. Abbott seldom thought of his son's feelings.

Now the trail boss explained Teddy's chores. "You're main job is help Mr. Thaddeus with the meals," he said. "When that's done you'll ride out and lend Ace a hand with the *remuda*."

After Mr. Cross left, Teddy asked Mr. Thaddeus, "What's a remuda?"

The cook replied, "That's the Texas word for the band of extra horses. Whenever the cowboy's horse gets tired from work, he goes to the remuda and ropes out a fresh one."

Teddy had seen sixteen-year-old Ace herding the loose horses. He knew Ace was the day wrangler, driving the remuda not far from the slow-moving Longhorns.

A second boy, Henry, had the job of night wrangler. He stayed with the horses all night, keeping them from straying away. Through the daytime, Henry slept in the rolling chuckwagon.

Teddy Abbott quickly learned his duties at the campfire.
Mr. Thaddeus showed him the tailgate on the wagon. It
dropped down to make a work table.

There the cook mixed biscuit dough. He cut biscuits and put them
into a Dutch oven on the fire to bake golden brown.

The usual cowboy meal was plenty of biscuits, beef, beans, and coffee.
If Mr. Thaddeus was in a good mood, he might make pies using dried
apples and sugar.

The cowboys worked hard to keep Mr. Thaddeus in a good mood.
They loved his pies.

Teddy liked being the cook's helper.
So did Shep. He got all the leftovers
and soon fattened up.

Working with Ace was a different matter. The horse wrangler was not kind to Teddy. He resented that Mr. Cross had sent a mere kid to help him with the remuda. Ace hardly spoke to Teddy at all.

For a week, the younger boy closely watched how Ace did his job, driving the horse herd. He saw him keep the animals bunched up. And he noted how Ace turned the lead horses to start the herd in another direction.

One evening at camp, Teddy said to Mr. Thaddeus: "Ace doesn't talk to me. He pretends I'm not even there. What should I do?"

The cook advised: "You'll just have to take it, young fellow. The men don't like anyone who complains. Remember that."

Teddy remembered and said nothing more about his problem with Ace.

A few days later Mr. Cross told Teddy to leave the remuda to Ace. Instead he should ride at the end of the cattle herd with Sam for a few days.

Some of the cattle were growing tired and lagged behind. It was important to keep the herd moving together.

Jogging along on Pete through the dust, Teddy Abbott exclaimed cheerfully: "Gee, Sam. This is fine. I'm almost a true cowboy."

"Not so fast, Master Teddy," replied a smiling Sam. "You still have a lot to learn. A man has to show that he's brave and will do the work. Only then can he call himself a cowboy. You still haven't earned your spurs."

By now Teddy understood what Sam meant. "I can't wear spurs on my boots yet," he said to himself. "First I gotta win respect of the trail crew."

June drifted by on the trail. The Abbott Longhorns moved steadily northward toward the Kansas boundary line.

Teddy had been sent back to the remuda as Ace's helper. Only now he kept his silence, trying as hard as he could to be a good wrangler.

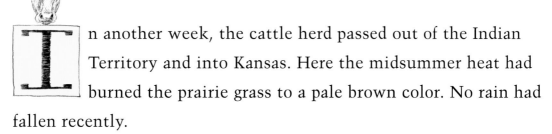

In another week, the cattle herd passed out of the Indian Territory and into Kansas. Here the midsummer heat had burned the prairie grass to a pale brown color. No rain had fallen recently.

Early one morning, Teddy was washing up the cowboys' tin plates and cups after breakfast. Mr. Cross had just given Sam orders for the day. Suddenly some Pawnees rode up to the chuckwagon.

The Indians told Mr. Cross that they were on their way west hunting buffalo. Their food supplies were low and they asked for a gift of beef. The trail boss agreed.

He had Sam bring in a young steer from the herd. The Pawnees were pleased. Then away they went, whooping and driving the steer ahead of them.

Vito Cross remarked: "Those Indians are friendly to us. It's worth a steer to keep them that way."

Not long after the Pawnee visit, Ace had an accident. His horse fell and threw him to the ground.

Teddy saw it happen. When he rode over, Ace was limping badly and his face was white.

"Do you want me to go for help?" Teddy asked.

"No!" replied the wrangler sharply. "It's just my leg. I'll be all right."

Teddy watched as the wounded Ace pulled himself up into the saddle. Both boys went back to herding the remuda.

When the sun began to set, they drove the horses to camp. Henry was waiting to start his duties as night wrangler.

Ace got off his horse. When his injured leg touched the ground, he cried out in pain. Then he fainted.

Shortly, Vito Cross brought Ace around, wiping his face with a wet cloth. "Your leg is badly broken," he told the boy.

"Tomorrow Sam will take you to the Kaw Indian Agency. They'll doctor your leg. After the drive is finished, Mr. Thaddeus and I will pick you up on our way back to Texas with the chuckwagon."

Then the trail boss asked Ace a question. "We're short a day wrangler now. Do you think Teddy can handle the remuda by himself?"

In a weak voice, Ace declared: "Yes sir, Mr. Cross. I'm sure he can. He's been doing right well lately and knows the job."

Teddy couldn't have been more surprised to hear that.

In the days that followed, Teddy Abbott settled into his new role as day wrangler. Mr. Thaddeus had to get along without him, but he didn't mind. The cook was glad to see Teddy enjoying himself with the horse work.

As the drive neared Nebraska and the Abbott ranch, the country grew drier. The sun came up hot each day, burning the short grass and blistering the cowboys.

Vito Cross was worried. At the campfire he said: "Men, the Longhorns are losing weight on this poor grass. And they are getting nervous and edgy because of the hot weather. You all know what that means."

The crew knew exactly what it meant. Only Teddy was unsure.

Later Mr. Thaddeus explained. "Teddy, the boss was talking about a stampede. That's the one thing all cowboys are afraid of."

"You see, those Longhorns, when they are worn out and hungry become easily frightened. Any loud noise, while the animals are sleeping on the bedground, can set them off."

"The whole herd will be up and running in just a few seconds. The men have to ride like fury in the dark. They try to turn the leaders and get the herd to run in a circle."

"Many a cowboy has been killed in a stampede. If a man's horse falls, he's likely to be trampled to death," concluded Mr. Thaddeus.

Crawling into his blankets, Teddy prayed he would never see a cattle stampede.

During the next several days, the Longhorns became harder to handle. Parts of the herd would start to break away, while others just came to a stop.

The men, on their tired and sweaty horses, did their best to keep the animals together and moving.

Sam rode out to the remuda to get a fresh horse. "Ain't cowboy life grand, Master Teddy?" he said with his usual smile.

At that moment, a hot and tired Teddy Abbott couldn't say whether he agreed with Sam or not.

The trail crew, with its herd of Texas Longhorns, was three days north of the Nebraska boundary when the weather changed.

A wind blew out of the west most of the day. By evening dark clouds gathered on the horizon. Smell of rain was in the air.

"Boys, looks like we are in for it tonight," warned Mr. Cross at the chuckwagon. "Everybody keep a horse tied up in case I call you out."

The trail boss sent several extra cowboys to circle the herd and sing songs. Their voices soothed the animals and made them less nervous. Henry was told to keep the remuda nearby, so riders could change horses fast.

Worried as he was at bedtime, Teddy managed to fall asleep under a heavy tarp. The last thing he heard was one of the cowboys singing:

Yippie-ti-yi-yo,
Get along little doggies.
You know Nebraska,
Will be your new home.

Sometime in the night, scattered raindrops began to pelt the canvas tarp. The next thing Teddy knew Mr. Thaddeus was shaking his shoulder.

"Get up quick," the cook told him. "The cowboys have already ridden out to the herd. The boss wants you to saddle Pete and go help Henry."

Teddy called for Shep. Flashes of lightening lit the night sky, so he was able to find the remuda. He saw poor Henry struggling to control the horses.

At that moment, a shattering crash of thunder rocked the bedground. In an instant, every Longhorn was up and running.

"Sta-a-am-pede!" yelled Vito Cross.

Shep barked furiously.

The lightning flashes gave young Teddy a perfect view of the ghostly scene. The cowboys raced beside the cattle. Vito Cross rode out front trying to turn and slow the leaders.

Suddenly a zigzag burst of yellow lightning struck the ground. Teddy rubbed his eyes, not believing what he saw. At the tip of every cow's horns appeared a bluish ball of fire.

Cowboys called it foxfire, a mysterious light seen in storms on the prairies.

The lightning frightened the horses. Now, they swerved away from the cattle and galloped into the darkness as a heavy rain began to fall.

Teddy and Shep followed them. Henry veered off chasing a single breakaway horse and was seen no more.

For the first time that night, Teddy Abbott
was truly scared. "Gosh agorry," he shouted at
Shep. "Is this remuda ever going to slow down?"
Shep had no answer for him.
So through the rain and blackness, the two of them
raced with the horse herd over the dismal and muddy plain.
Teddy had never before felt so alone. But he knew his duty as a
wrangler, and that was to stay with
the horses no matter what!

At dawn the animals finally came to a stop and began to graze. By then, Teddy was half asleep in the saddle.

Suddenly he jerked awake. Circling, he gently turned the horses around and started them back toward the Longhorn herd.

"Shep, boy. Where are you?" Teddy called. But no bark answered him. Feeling panic, he hollered again and again. Shep was missing!

Two hours later, some of the Abbott cowboys rode up. One of them said, "Man o' man. Are we glad to find you, Teddy. We got the cattle stopped and quieted down. But none of us expected to see these horses again."

The cowboys, without another word, took over the remuda and made a fast drive back to camp.

Mr. Thaddeus had biscuits and a tin plate of beans waiting for Teddy. The boy was so sad he could hardly eat. No one had praised him for saving the remuda. And worst of all, Shep was gone.

Three days after the stampede, the cattle herd reached the Abbott ranch. The long hard drive ended.

Mr. Abbott paid off the crew. With their wages, the cowboys headed for town to celebrate. All of them, even Sam, left without telling Teddy good-bye.

Vito Cross and Mr. Thaddeus stayed behind to pack the chuckwagon for their trip home. They looked for Teddy and found him alone in the barn. He was sitting on an upturned bucket with his head in his hands.

"Why so sad, fella'?" Mr. Cross asked.

"I guess I'm sorry the drive is over," Teddy replied. "But I'm most sorry 'cause the cowboys don't seem to think what I did was worth anything."

"Where'd you get that idea, Teddy?" the trail boss said kindly. "From the moment they found you on the plains driving the remuda back, you were accepted as one of them. You survived the stampede and the storm and proved you could do a wrangler's work."

His words and a smile from Mr. Thaddeus made Teddy feel better.

Later, Teddy faced his father. Edward Abbott saw that his son had changed. He no longer looked sickly, but stood taller and seemed older. The cattle drive had been good for him.

"Teddy, Mr. Cross told me how you saved the horse herd. I'm very proud of you, young man." That was the first time Teddy could remember getting his father's approval. A big grin lit up his face.

The morning after the cowboys left for town, Teddy walked out on the trail. Sadly, he stood for a long time looking south toward Texas.

Then he saw a skinny dog hobbling toward him, dragging a hind leg. It was Shep! Soon the dog was in his arms licking Teddy's hands as he'd first done on the Red River. It was hard to tell which of the two was happier.

When the pair got back to the ranch house, Teddy had another surprise. The whole crew was there on horseback in front of the porch, talking with Mr. Abbott.

"Well, here's our hero of the stampede," announced Sam. "Teddy, we all chipped in and bought you something. Here's your first pair of spurs. You sure earned them!"

On that day, Teddy Abbott was the proudest boy in Nebraska.

Cowboy Words

BAY—a popular horse color, different shades of red-brown

BEDGROUND—an area where a herd of cattle lies down for the night

CHISHOLM TRAIL—most famous of the old cattle trails leading northward from Texas

CHUCKWAGON—special wagon used by range cooks when preparing meals on the trail

CORRAL—pens used to hold livestock

DUTCH OVEN—a round iron pot with a flat lid, used for campfire baking

FOXFIRE—a strange bluish light that appears at the tip of cows' horns during an electrical storm

LONGHORNS—wild Texas cattle with a wide spread of horns sometimes reaching six feet

NECKERCHIEF—worn by cowboys around the neck to be pulled up over the nose in dusty or snowy weather

REMUDA—a Spanish word used in Texas for a herd of spare horses

SPUR—metal band with wheel or star strapped to cowboy boots and used by riders to signal the horse

STAMPEDE—a runaway herd of cattle dreaded by all cowmen

TRAIL BOSS—the headman on a cattle drive

WRANGLER—a man or boy in charge of horses

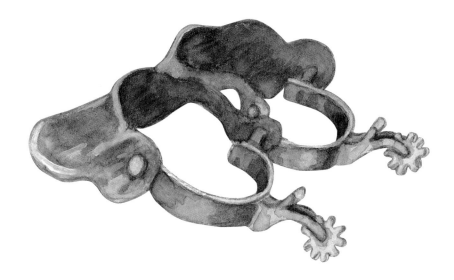

Sources

E. C. "Teddy" Abbott spent fifty years of his life as a cowboy. He made three more trail drives, the last one to Montana in 1883.

In 1939, an elderly Teddy published his book, *We Pointed Them North: Recollections of a Cowpuncher.* In it, he mentions that his friend on the Chisholm Trail, Sam Bass, was "a nice fellow, always very kind to me." Later, Sam became an outlaw and was killed by Texas Rangers.

In his book, Teddy Abbott gives only a few details of his childhood cattle drive. In telling this story, events common to the Chisholm Trail were added that fit with the time and place.

Standard references are J. Frank Dobie, *The Longhorns* (1941) and Charles M. Russell, *Trails Plowed Under* (1927). Russell, a western artist, and Teddy Abbott planned to do a book together on cowboys. But Russell died before the project could be started.

Teddy Abbott

Circa 1919

C M Russell